Bloomers Island®

Violet

and the
Eggplant Painting Problem

**CYNTHIA WYLIE and
COURTNEY CARBONE**

Illustrations by KATYA LONGHI

the HiDDeN ForeST

MAGICAL MeADOW

HONEYBUNCH FLOWER GARDEN

RODALE KiDS
RODALEKIDS.COM

An imprint of Rodale Books
733 Third Avenue
New York, NY 10017
Visit us online at RodaleKids.com.

Text & Art © 2018 Bloomers! Edutainment, LLC

Rodale Kids books may be purchased for business or
promotional use or for special sales. For information,
please e-mail: RodaleKids@Rodale.com

Printed in China

Manufactured by RRD Asia 201804

Book design by Christina Gaugler and Ariana Abud

Library of Congress Cataloging-in-Publication Data is on file with the publisher.

ISBN 978-1-63565-112-6 paperback

Distributed to the trade by Macmillan

10 9 8 7 6 5 4 3 2 1 paperback

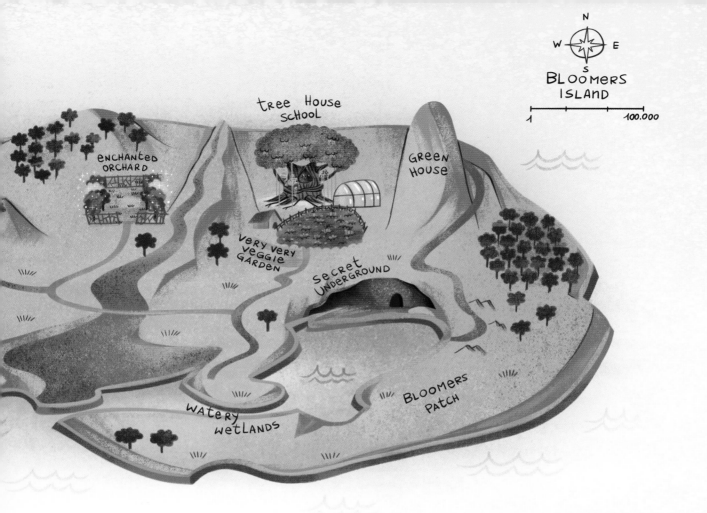

Dedicated to all the dreamers and artists and kids who love purple. Like me.

—C.W.

For budding green thumbs everywhere, that their hearts and minds may grow
as magnificently as their gardens.

—C.B.C.

To my amazing husband and family for supporting and believing in me on this beautiful journey.
Much love and thanks to everyone who follows my books and illustrations.

—K.L.

It was the start of a new school year on Bloomers Island. The headmaster of Tree House School, **Professor Sage**, was excited to teach his students, the Bloomers, all about the *wonderful world of gardening*.

"I have a special announcement today, class," Professor Sage said. "We are going to have a class contest. Each of you will grow your own vegetable, and in several weeks, we will see who has grown the best one."

Violet was always up for a challenge! She knew at once that she wanted to grow eggplants. Eggplants—big, dark purple veggies—had always been her favorite.

Violet's hand shot up into the air.

"Professor, I would like to grow eggplants," she began. "But . . . why are they called eggplants when they don't look anything like eggs?"

"Excellent question, Violet," Professor Sage said,
smiling and handing her a packet of seeds.
"I look forward to hearing the answer during
your final presentation!"

Violet was naturally curious, so she couldn't wait to find out the answer. That night, she went to the library and read all about eggplants.

Seeing the many different pictures in her book gave her an idea. Instead of keeping a written log, she could paint pictures of the eggplants to track her progress!

The next day, Violet went down to the garden with the other Bloomers. But instead of planting her seeds in the ground like her friends, she planted them in small clay pots like the books suggested.

Back in the girls' dormitory that afternoon, Violet set the pots next to her artist's easel by the window. She would keep the pots inside until her plants were ready to move to the garden.

In the meantime, she got started on her painting!

The eggplants slowly began to grow. It was hard for Violet to be patient while waiting, but painting was fun and helped her pass the time.

Soon, she had a whole collection of beautiful paintings—and a bunch of small plants ready to be moved to the garden!

In the garden, Violet picked a sunny spot with sandy soil. She planted the seedlings far apart so they would have lots of room to grow. Next, she used compost to add nutrients to the soil.

The next morning, beautiful white and purple flowers appeared on Violet's plants! She couldn't wait to paint them. She ran all the way upstairs to her room.

But when she got there, she saw that she was all out of purple paint!

Violet did not know what to do. She sadly looked out her window at her plants below. Then she spotted something—or rather, *someone!* **The Snail Mailman** was slowly making his way toward the school.

"Mr. Snail Mailman," Violet cried. "I need to order more paint as soon as possible!"

"I see," he replied. "If I go as fast as I can, I can get you new paints by next month."

Violet clenched her hands in frustration. That was too long. She would have to come up with another plan.

Violet went to Professor Sage's office, and explained the situation.

"What do I do?" she asked. "In another month, my plants will be rotten! I'll never win the Best Vegetable award."

"Don't worry, Violet," he replied from on top of a bookshelf ladder. "You are one of my most creative students. I'm sure you'll find a solution to your problem."

"Maybe this will help," he said, handing her an arts & crafts book.

Violet leafed through the arts & crafts book with her friends. Suddenly, she saw a recipe for making homemade paint.

It was easy!

All she needed was water, flour, salt, and dye.

She could find everything in the school kitchen except for purple dye.

Luckily, the book also had a recipe for making homemade dye!

All she needed was to find purple berries.

During recess the next day, Violet and her friends went on a berry hunt near the school.

"Be on the lookout for blackberries," Violet told them, "They have purple juice."

"I don't want to walk too far," Rosey Posey said. "It's too hot."

"Blackberries need hot weather to ripen and get juicy," Violet replied.

Suddenly, Lilly waved wildly to the others. She had spotted a blackberry bush straight ahead.

"That's not too far," said Rosey Posey. "Come on! Let's go pick some blackberries!"

After school, Violet and her friends brought their basket of berries into the kitchen for a squishing party. It was messy, but lots of fun. Even neat-and-clean Rosey Posey had a great time!

Violet strained the blackberry seeds
and mixed the purple juice with flour,
salt, and water. In no time, she
had lots of smushy, gushy purple
paint! Finally, she could get back
to work on her project.

Violet's eggplants continued to grow big and strong. Within a week, they were ready to be picked. She selected the **biggest** and **longest** eggplant of all to present to her class the next day.

"Long ago," Violet began. "Eggplants were egg-shaped and yellowish-white in color. They got their name because early explorers thought they looked like eggs."

The whole class laughed as they nibbled on roasted eggplant slices.

"But nowadays, when we hear 'eggplant,' most of us think of a plump purple vegetable," Violet continued. "And that is exactly what I grew!"

Violet showed the class her fantastic paintings. Everyone *ooh*-ed and *ahh*-ed.

"Congratulations, Violet!" Professor Sage said, proudly.

"You really made this project your own! You have truly earned the Most Creative Gardener award."

Violet beamed, as everyone gave her a hearty round of applause.

She had done it!

Violet's

Excellent Eggplant "Fries"

PREP TIME: 10 minutes | **YIELD:** about 40 fries

Dip in Big Red's Favorite Ketchup from *Big Red and the Terrible Tomato Hornworm* and draw a masterpiece on your plate!

Ingredients

1 medium eggplant, peeled
⅓ cup flour
½ teaspoon kosher salt
½ cup bread crumbs
¼ cup grated Parmesan cheese
2 large eggs, beaten
Cooking oil spray

Directions

1. With a grownup's supervision, preheat the oven to 400 degrees F.
2. Cut the eggplant into ½-inch wide by 2-inch long sticks.
3. Line up 3 bowls. Place the flour and salt in the first bowl, the beaten eggs in the second, and the bread crumbs and cheese in the third.
4. Dip the eggplant sticks in the flour mixture, followed by the egg, and then in the bread crumbs.
5. Place on a cooking rack over a baking sheet and lightly spray with cooking oil spray.
6. Bake for 25 to 30 minutes or until soft inside and golden outside.
7. Place on a paper towel for 5 minutes to cool before enjoying!